T0378543

BE YOUR **OWN** BOSS

PLAN A YARD-WORK BUSINESS

STEPHANE HILLARD

PowerKiDS press
New York

Published in 2021 by The Rosen Publishing Group, Inc.
29 East 21st Street, New York, NY 10010

First Edition

Portions of this work were originally authored by Emma Carlson Berne and published as *Run Your Own Yard-Work Business*. All new material in this edition authored by Stephane Hillard.

Editor: Elizabeth Krajnik
Book Design: Reann Nye

Photo Credits: Cover Yobro10/iStock / Getty Images Plus/Getty Images; series art stas11/Shutterstock.com; p. 5 Craig Barritt/Getty Images Entertainment/Getty Images; p. 7 ER_09/Shutterstock.com; p. 9 Jodie Griggs/The Image Bank/Getty Images; p. 11 Vitaly Korovin/Shutterstock.com; p. 13 Tom Werner/DigitalVision/Getty Images; p. 15 praetorianphoto/E+/Getty Images; p. 17 monkeybusinessimages/iStock / Getty Images Plus/Getty Images; p. 19 HMVart/E+/Getty Images; p. 21 Monty Rakusen/Cultura/Getty Images; p. 22 Jose Luis Pelaez Inc/DigitalVision/Getty Images.

Library of Congress Cataloging-in-Publication Data

Names: Hillard, Stephane, author.
Title: Plan a yard-work business / Stephane Hillard.
Description: New York : PowerKids Press, [2021] | Series: Be your own boss | Includes index.
Identifiers: LCCN 2020003204 | ISBN 9781725319097 (paperback) | ISBN 9781725319110 (library binding) | ISBN 9781725319103 (6 pack)
Subjects: LCSH: Lawn care industry–Juvenile literature. | Lawns–Juvenile literature. | Money-making projects for children–Juvenile literature. | Entrepreneurship–Juvenile literature.
Classification: LCC SB433.27 .H55 2021 | DDC 635.9/647–dc23
LC record available at https://lccn.loc.gov/2020003204

Manufactured in the United States of America

CPSIA Compliance Information: Batch #CSPK20. For Further Information contact Rosen Publishing, New York, New York at 1-800-237-9932.

CONTENTS

YOUNG ENTREPRENEURS

Have you ever wanted a new bike but didn't have enough money for it? Or maybe you want to save money to travel the world when you're older. You could start your own business to make and save money. Then you'd be a young entrepreneur. An entrepreneur is a person who starts a business and is willing to possibly lose money in order to make money.

This book will show you the steps to follow to plan and start your own business, including making a business plan, creating a **budget**, advertising, and more. In time, you'll be able to enjoy your business's profits.

Bella Weems-Lambert wanted to buy a car when she turned 16 years old. When she was 14 years old, after saving $350 from babysitting jobs, she began making and selling **customizable** jewelry. Her business is called Origami Owl.

SUPPLY AND DEMAND

To decide what kind of business to start, look around your community. Successful businesses supply a demand, or want or need, for their **customers**.

Before you start your business, make a list of products or services you think you could provide. Then do some **research**. You can avoid **competition** by choosing a product or service that isn't already being provided. What jobs are people doing for themselves that you might be able to do for them?

Starting a yard-work business is great for young entrepreneurs. You can shovel people's sidewalks, rake their leaves, weed their gardens, mow their lawns, or trim their bushes.

GOOD BUSINESS

If there's another yard-work business in town, you can offer different services or different rates. That way you won't be competing.

The yard work you can do depends on the season and where you live. In the fall you can rake people's leaves.

CREATING A BUSINESS PLAN

Before you start your yard-work business, you'll need to create a business plan. This plan outlines where, when, and how you'll run your business. First, you should decide which yard-work services you'd like to provide.

The "where" of your business plan is easy. You'll run your business in your customers' yards. The "when" will depend on when your customers need you and when you're able to work.

Finally, think about how you will run your business. Make a list of tools you will need, such as a rake and a shovel. Then think about which tools you already own or can borrow and which you might need to purchase.

GOOD BUSINESS

Talk to your parents about your business hours. Will you be allowed to work after school? Or will they only allow you to work on weekends? You can **schedule** appointments or offer your services on the spot.

If you're going to mow people's lawns, you'll need a lawn mower. You might also consider getting a weed whacker and a broom or a leaf blower to clean up the grass clippings.

EXPENSES AND BUDGETING

Your yard-work business, like all other businesses, will have expenses. Expenses are costs that arise throughout the course of doing business. Creating a budget for your yard-work business will allow you to keep track of your expenses.

To create your budget, make a list of everything you'll need to start and run your yard-work business. Check how much money you have saved. Do you have enough saved to run your business for a few weeks? If not, you'll need to borrow some money, most likely from your parents. Then you'll need to make a plan to repay them.

GOOD BUSINESS

To know how much to charge your customers for your services, add up how much money you've put into your business and your other expenses for one month. Then add how much of a profit you'd like to make. Divide that number by the number of services you think you can provide in one month.

Alex's Yard-Care Services: Fee

Money put into business	$350
Monthly expenses	$250
Total:	$600
Profit	10%
10% of $600	$60
$600 + $60	$660
Number of services per month	24
$660 ÷ 24	$27.50 per service

Even small things, such as markers to make signs, cost money. Be sure to add these to your budget.

THE IMPORTANCE OF ADVERTISING

Advertising is how you'll tell people you're starting a yard-work business. You can advertise by telling people in your neighborhood—which is called word of mouth—by making flyers or signs, or by putting an ad in your local newspaper.

On your advertising **materials** you should put the services you offer, how much you charge for each service, your business hours, and your phone number. You should also put whether you'll bring your own tools or if you'll need to use your customers' tools.

After you've made your flyers and signs, you can hang them up in your community or put them in your neighbors' mailboxes.

GOOD BUSINESS

Ask your parents if they'd post an ad for your business on their social media pages, such as Facebook and Instagram. They may let you make a page for your business as well.

If it's in your budget, you can make a website for your yard-work business. Make sure to check if that's OK with your parents first.

HIRING EMPLOYEES

Hiring **employees** will make running your yard-work business easier. You'll also be able to do yard-work jobs more quickly, which means you'll be able to schedule more jobs and make more of a profit. You'll need to figure out how your employees can be most helpful. Will you go to different job locations or will you work together at the same job location?

You'll have to pay your employees. You can pay them an hourly wage or you can pay them a percentage of the profits. Your employees may work harder if they know they'll get more money.

Having a friend help you with your yard work may make the time pass by quicker. You may even have a fun time shoveling the snow with them!

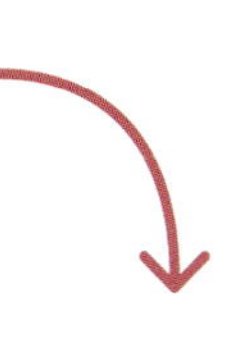

GETTING ORGANIZED

Soon after you advertise your yard-work business, calls will start to come in. It's important to be **professional** on the phone. Greet your customers pleasantly, stating the name of your business. Ask your customer about what service they'd like to book and when, and ask for their name, phone number, and address.

You should know about how many jobs or hours of work you can handle each day. Look at your schedule and see when you can fit the customer in. Tell your customer how long the job will take and how much it will cost. You should also tell them when you'll expect payment.

GOOD BUSINESS

Keep track of your yard-work jobs in a planner. If you forget you're scheduled to rake someone's leaves, that customer might not ask you to work for them again. They may also tell their friends that you didn't show up.

A paper planner can help you keep track of your jobs. You can also keep track of your jobs on your computer or phone by using a calendar app that can be shared with your employees.

GATHERING SUPPLIES

Running a yard-work business is expensive. Many of the tools you need, such as a lawn mower or leaf blower, are large and costly. To save money, you can ask to rent or borrow these items from your parents. If your customers have these tools, you can arrange to use theirs.

Make a list of other tools you'll need. These might include gardening gloves, a reusable water bottle, sunscreen and a hat, and small bills to make change. Once you've gathered these items, you'll be ready to get to work. If you keep your supplies organized, you won't waste valuable time searching for them before a job.

Tools, such as a shovel and rake, don't cost much money. You can load your smaller supplies into a wheelbarrow to take to the job location.

TIME TO WORK!

Now that you've created your business plan, made a budget, advertised, hired employees, scheduled jobs, and gathered your supplies, it's time to get to work!

When you arrive at the job location, greet your customer by saying something like, "Hi! I'm Andy of Andy's Yard-Care Services. I'm here for your 2:00 lawn mowing service."

Confirm what kind of work you're doing, how long it should take, and how much you charge for your services. Before you leave the job location, make sure the customer has looked over your work and is satisfied. After you've been paid and paid your employees, you can enjoy the profits!

GOOD BUSINESS

Keep track of each job in a notebook. Write down where the job was, the type of service you provided, how long it took, and how much you were paid.

If you do good work, your customers will want you to work for them again. The more repeat customers you have, the more money you'll make. Repeat customers can also tell new customers about your yard-work business.

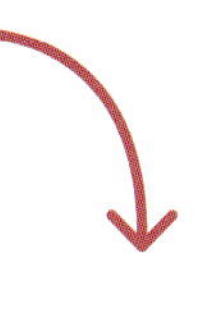

BUSINESS CHECKLIST

- Address a community need
- Create a business plan
- Create a budget
- Purchase advertising materials
- Advertise your yard-work business
- Hire employees
- Schedule yard-work jobs
- Gather your supplies
- Provide yard-work services
- Pay your employees
- Enjoy the profits

GLOSSARY

budget: A plan used to decide the amount of money that can be spent and how it will be spent.

competition: A person or group you're trying to succeed against.

customer: Someone who buys goods or services from a business.

customizable: Able to be changed to fit the needs or requirements of a person, business, etc.

employee: A person who's paid to work for another.

material: Matter from which something is made or can be made.

professional: Having or showing a quality appropriate in a profession.

research: Careful study that is done to find and report new knowledge about something.

schedule: To plan for a certain time.

INDEX

WEBSITES

Due to the changing nature of Internet links, PowerKids Press has developed an online list of websites related to the subject of this book. This site is updated regularly. Please use this link to access the list:
www.powerkidslinks.com/byoboss/yardwork